Pinkalicious™

and the
Pink Drink

by Victoria Kann

HARPER FESTIVAL
An Imprint of HarperCollinsPublishers

To Sallie
—V.K.

The author gratefully acknowledges
the artistic and editorial contributions
of Barry Gott and Susan Hill.

HarperFestival is an imprint of HarperCollins Publishers.

Pinkalicious: Pinkalicious and the Pink Drink
Copyright © 2010 by Victoria Kann

PINKALICIOUS and all related logos and characters
are trademarks of Victoria Kann. Used with permission.

Based on the HarperCollins book *Pinkalicious* written by
Victoria Kann and Elizabeth Kann, illustrated by Victoria Kann.

Library of Congress catalog card number: 2009941833
ISBN 978-0-06-192732-4

Book design by John Sazaklis
18   SCP   30 29 28 27
❖
First Edition

It was a sunny day, too hot to play.
I was blowing bubbles in the shade.

That made me think of the giant bubblegum machine at the toy store. I ran inside to check my piggy bank.

It was empty!

I wanted a gumball. I wanted twenty gumballs. I wanted thirty-five gumballs, pink ones!

But how could I get the money to buy them?

Mommy said, "Let's have a lemonade stand!"
"Pink lemonade!" I said. "Pink, pink, pink!"
Mommy got out the pitcher and the sugar and the lemons.
"I know how!" I said. "I'll do it myself!"

I put the sugar and the water into the pitcher.
squeezed the lemons. I stirred it all together.
It was yummy. But it wasn't pink.

I opened the fridge. I didn't find any pink lemons, but I found some other pinkish things: pink grapefruit, pink watermelon, pink frosting, and a bowlful of purplicious beets.

I put all of them in the pitcher and I stirred it all up.

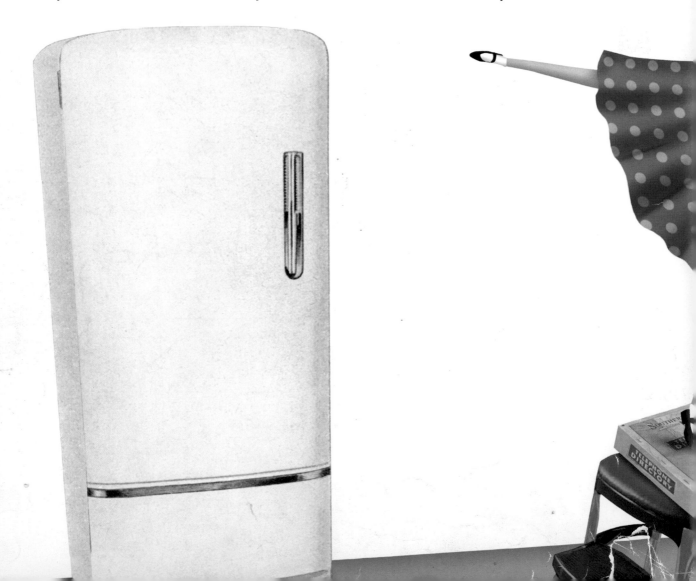

My little brother, Peter, helped me put up my pink lemonade stand. I let him try the lemonade for free.

"Weird," said Peter. "Kind of chewy. I like it."

Mr. Peabody came by and gave me a quarter.

My first real customer!

Mr. Peabody made a face. "It's definitely missing something," he said. "Either that, or it has too much of something else."

I had an idea. "The sweeter, the better," I said.
I ran and got the honey bear and squeezed the honey in.
Peter stirred and—oh no! He knocked over the pitcher!
"I'm sorry, Pinkalicious!" he said. "Don't get mad!"

I got mad.

"That's easy to fix, Pinkalicious. We'll make some more," said Mommy

I started to get out the pink grapefruit, pink watermelon, pink frosting, and purplicious beets.

"What's all that?" Mommy asked.

"All that's how to make it pink," I told her.

Mommy said, "How about we just use one thing to make it pink this time." And she pulled out some strawberries.

It wasn't as exciting or as lumpy as the first batch, but it was still beautiful pink lemonade. I sold the whole pitcher in no time flat.

I went to the toy store with my lemonade stand money. Six quarters, four dimes, five nickels, and ten pennies.

Nine gumballs, pink ones! Eight for me and one for Peter.

Peter looked sad. I gave him three and kept six. Peter still looked sad. I stuffed one gumball in my mouth, kept four, and gave four to Peter. "Even-Steven!" Peter said. He was very happy.

Gumballs don't last forever, and my piggy bank is empty again.

Maybe tomorrow I'll have a bake sale. I can make pink cupcakes.